TEDDY
On Safari

Teddy was puzzled, he told his friends so.
"What's going on? Does anyone know?
There's a secret for sure, and I've got to find out,
What all the mystery and whispering's about!"

Just then the 'phone rang.
"It's a long distance call.
        Hurry up!" cried Mother,
        "and come to the hall.
It's your uncle from Africa -
Game Warden Bear,
        He wants all you young bears
        to visit there!"

The next week the bears
were so busy all day,
     Getting passports
     and tickets to go far away.

"Let's sit on each suitcase," Teddy said with a grin
     "It's a bit of a squash getting everything in!"

They checked-in at the airport, and then said goodbye.
Their plane looked so big, could it really fly?

They took-off from the runway - the trip had begun.
"Hurrah!" cheered the bears. "This will be fun."

The flight was so long, it took almost a day,
But the bears knew that Africa was a very long way.

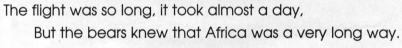

When at last the plane landed, all four Teddies ran,
To meet Uncle Bear, in his Game Warden's Van.
"You'll be tired," he beamed, "after such a long ride."
"Not a bit!" yelled the bears, as they clambered inside.

The airport and buildings were soon left behind.
On through grasslands the road seemed to wind.
"Was that a giraffe?" the bears squealed in delight.
"Look zebras!" laughed uncle. "Let's give them a fright!"

Uncle's Game Warden Van was striped black and white,
  It was painted that way to keep out of sight.
"We'll get close to the animals, as close as we dare,
  You must keep very quiet, and take care."

Uncle told the four friends, "We should head for home.
The sun sinks so fast here, it's no place to roam!"
As darkness fell, strange sounds they heard.
Was that noise a lion, or simply a bird?

ncle said with a grin, "You'll be safe as can be,
In my Game Warden's Lodge, high up in this tree."
ery soon the Teddies were tucked up for the night,
Dreaming of adventures to come, when it's light.

At first light of day, what a hullabaloo,
    Hyena's, zebras and pink flamingoes,
Each morning they came for a drink at sunrise,
    Right next to the tree-house. What a surprise!

The Teddies crept out on the platform to see,
    Elephants and lions, as close as can be.
"This water-hole's famous," said uncle with pride.
    "Sit here and watch, I'll bring breakfast outside!"

"It's still very early, the day's just begun,
      You must dress in light clothes, and wear hats in the sun."
How uncle laughed, when at last they were ready.
      "Here's a badge for you all, that says Game Warden Ted

Next they heard uncle calling, "Be as quick as you can.
Stop what you're doing and run for the van.
There's a fierce looking rhino heading this way.
He seems rather angry. I don't think we'll stay!"

The bears hung on tight, as the van drove off fast.
  "Oh, no!" gasped Teddy, "he's seen us drive past!"
Uncle shouted, "I'm going as fast as I can."
  But the rhino was faster and caught up with the van.

SMASH! went his horn into the van's side.
    The Teddies looked round for somewhere to hide.

Uncle jammed on the brakes and the van stood quite still,
    But the rhino charged on and ran over the hill.

"Wow, that was close!" uncle said with a smile.
"I'll turn the van round, he'll be back in a while!"
So they crossed a wide river, left the rhino behind,
But swimming towards them - what did they find?

"Crocodiles!" Teddy yelled, then turned to see,
A large herd of hippos that looked so friendly.
Uncle parked on the bank, "It's quite safe to get out.
The young ones will come if you give them a shout."

Baby hippos came out of the water to play,
    "This is sure to be fun," Teddy cried, "can we stay?"
They dived in the river, then splashed mud around,
    Rode on the big hippos, but were quite safe and sound.